For Kathleen Scott M.C.
For Frances C.G.

Library of Congress Cataloging in Publication Data

Cecil, Mirabel.   Cora the crow.
Summary: When they discover their favorite elm trees
have been cut down, Cora and the other crows are
forced to search for a new place to nest.
[1.   Crows—Fiction]   I.   Gascoigne, Christina,
1938 or 9-   II.   Title.
PZ7.C2998Co   [E]   79-22538
ISBN 0-07-010320-8

Text © 1980 Mirabel Cecil
Illustrations © 1980 Christina Gascoigne
Printed in Italy
Published and distributed in the United States
of America 1980 by McGraw-Hill Book Company,
1221 Avenue of the Americas, New York, N.Y. 10020
First published in Great Britain 1980 by
Methuen/Walker Books

1 2 3 4 5 6 7 8 9   8 7 6 5 4 3 2 1 0

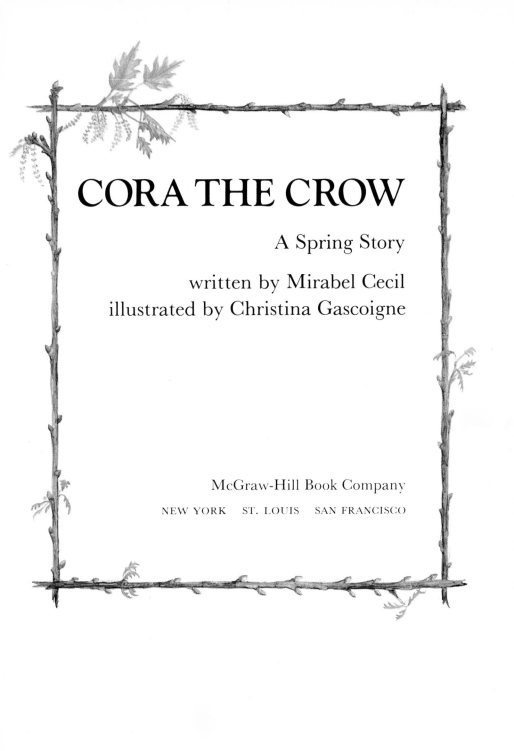

CORA THE CROW

A Spring Story

written by Mirabel Cecil
illustrated by Christina Gascoigne

McGraw-Hill Book Company

NEW YORK   ST. LOUIS   SAN FRANCISCO

EVERY SPRING, as soon as winter was really over, Cora and the other crows flew back to the beautiful old elm trees where they always built their nests.

The people who lived nearby knew that it would be a good summer if they saw the crows nesting high in the treetops.

But one year when the crows came back...

…none of their favorite trees were standing!

"CAW!" cried the crows.

Tree trunks were lying all over the ground. A burly man was chopping the branches into logs.

"Wheeouw … wheeouw…," whined a chain saw in the distance.

The crows looked sadly around.

"Where shall we build our nests now?"
wondered the unhappy crows.

"We must start looking at once!" said Cora.

So she and her friend Zuk flew off to search.

Soon they were back, full of excitement. They had found a really special grove.

"You'll love it!" exclaimed Cora.

"Tall trees!" cried Zuk.

"Lovely breeze!"

"Plenty of space!"

The other crows followed Cora and Zuk.

All the crows were impressed when they saw the new trees. It was early in the spring, so the birds could see many good spots in the bare branches for their nests. They didn't notice that a few strange crows were flying about.

Suddenly, a whole flock of other crows zoomed in on them. "These trees are ours! We got here first! Get off!" They screamed.

Before they knew what was happening,
Cora and her friends found themselves
under attack.

Feathers flew . . . beaks clashed!

Rooccoco, the oldest bird, was hit on the head by a piece of flying bark. He ordered his birds to retreat.

Cora felt that the fight had been her fault—she should have made sure that there were no birds already nesting in the trees. She worriedly put a plaster on old Rooccoco's wound, and she and Zuk wove him a comfortable stretcher from plaited grass and sticks.

By the time they finished the air ambulance, it was late and cold. The crows had to find another place for the night.

"Let's fly to the town nearby," suggested
Rooccoco sleepily.

So all the crows flew to the town and perched around the market square.

The next day they decided to stay in the town until Rooccoco recovered. The young crows were delighted. They liked bathing in the fountain and eating the food left over from the market stands. But the older crows shook their heads.

"We can't stay here. The lights would keep the nestlings awake—and us, too. We've never lived in a town and we won't start now."

So Cora, Zuk, and some of the other crows
went searching for a new home.

Birds were already nesting
everywhere. Some of their
eggs had even hatched.

The woodpeckers had
hollowed out a nest in a
tree and lined it with
wood chips.

The robins had filled an old
kettle with leaves for their nest.

The woodpigeons
had built an
untidy nest in
a tree.

The little hedgesparrow's nest
was neatly lined with warm straw.

The spring days were passing.
Where could the crows
lay their eggs? Cora and
her friends
were very troubled.

One day when they were out searching,
Cora and Zuk heard a terrible row.

"Help! Help!"
cheeped the little
hedgesparrow.
The crows flew
closer. A fierce
hawk was carrying
off the little
hedgesparrow's mate.
"We'll rescue your mate!"
cried Cora and Zuk.

They flew off as fast
as they could after the
hawk, calling to the other
crows to come with them.

The crows caught up with the hawk just as he was about to land in a field with the little sparrow. The hawk was amazed to find himself surrounded by diving crows.

Again and again the crows flew at the cruel bird, until at last he had to drop the hedgesparrow.

The tiny bird
flew away at
once.

The hedgesparrows were so grateful
that they decided to help the crows
find somewhere to nest.

"I'm sure we've seen a good place
very near here!" cheeped one little
hedgesparrow.

"If only we could remember where it is!"
cheeped the other.

But finally they did remember, and they led
the crows to a cluster of beautiful old
walnut trees.

This time Cora made sure that
there were no other birds in the trees.

All the crows agreed that they would
be quite happy in the walnut trees, even
though the trees weren't very tall.

Cora and Zuk built their nest,
and as soon as their eggs were
hatched, the little hedgesparrow
came to visit them.

Her troubles over, Cora sometimes sang
to her nestlings:

"Hush a-bye birdies, on the tree top!
When the wind blows, the nest will rock!
If the bough breaks, the nest will fall—
And down will come nest, birdies and all."

The little birds just snuggled cozily
together, untroubled by their
mother's song.

E -0   Cecil, Mirabel
C

Cora the crow

DATE			